In Tune with God

PRAYERS AND REFLECTIONS

In Tune with God

PRAYERS AND REFLECTIONS

Jeevan Babu

2011

In Tune with God: Prayers and Reflections – Published by Rev Dr. Ashish Amos of the Indian Society for Promoting Christian Knowledge (ISPCK), Post Box 1585, 1654 Madarsa Road Kashmere Gate, Delhi-110006.

Cover Page Designed by Mr. John Rajan, Bangalore

ISBN: 978-81-8465-138-6

Laser typeset by **ISPCK,** Post Box 1585, 1654 Madarsa Road, Kashmere Gate, Delhi-110006 Tel: 23866322, 23866323 e-mail–ashish@ispck.org.in • ella@ispck.org.in website-www.ispck.org.

Dedicated to

The Family and Ministry of

ISPCK, Delhi

CONTENTS

ACKNOWLEDGEMENTS

One day as I was meditating on several BLESSINGS OF GOD, a thought came to my mind to do a series of prayers through which people can reflect on several blessings of God and discover the Grace of God. The result is this book "In tune with God" It took little longer time for me to bring the material to the shape as you have it in your hands.

First I thank God who inspires me and gives space and time to do these reflections. I thank Fr.Clarance D'Souza Vice Principal, St. Joseph's College, Bangalore and Miss. Jyothsna English Lecturer, St. Joseph's College, Bangalore, who went through the pages for any corrections in the language. I thank Rev. Dr. Ashish Amos and Mrs. Ella of ISPCK, Delhi, for their encouragement and for publishing this work for the glory of God.

I always begin to think of a new book after I see the last book released. As you remember my last book was 'Discovering God's Love through pain and faith' which was the experience and the result of transplantation of Kidney for me. As my son Kiran kidney donor and I have recovered very fast and started working on Prayers. It was a busy time of shifting from one small church to little bigger church. Yet God gave me enough strength and solemn time to reflect on themes I presented before you. I thank my family members Mrs. Kasthuri Jeevan my beloved wife, my son Kiran and my daughter Miss Keerthi, for their interventions, suggestions and granting me free time from domestic duties. Thank you for reading and using these prayers in your life and pass it on the experience and blessings to others.

FOREWORD

One of the beautiful descriptions of prayer is- 'Prayer is love'. It is love expressed in speech and love expressed in silence. In other words, prayer is a meeting of two lovers. The end of prayer is the love of God. Hence, in a wonderful way prayer and to pray is to be in the presence of someone we love and who loves us.

The Rev. Jeevan Babu has beautifully brought out these facets of what is and what prayer can be, in this book 'In Tune with God' with a beautiful spread of over a collection of 73 of them. They make reading simple and yet reflect a deep desire to recognize, to experience the love, blessings, care and protection of the Lord. The prayers and the reflections are written in simple and readable language with a genial flow off and on of poetical naunces. They beautifuly reflect the life experiences of Rev. Jeevan Babu, bringing to light his rich and varied experiemnces as a pastor. One cannot fail to find the spiritual depths of insights they contain.

May these beautiful prayerful reflections meant for all times, seasons, stages and moments in life not only make a pleasent reading but much more help one to experience the lovable, compassionate and living God! of a God and Lord who embraces us in His care, irrespective of who we are! May they help us to sense the constant touch of the Divine in the sage of our lives.

It is my prayer that the Lord bless this wonderful work, which infact is the fifteenth published work of Rev. Jeevan Babu! May it be for the greater glory of God and be a blessing for peace, joy, hope and love for our sisters and brothers.

Fr. Clarence D'Sauza SJ
Vice-Principal
St. Joseph's College (Autonomous)
Langford Road
Bangalore - 560027

1. I WISH TO PRAY

I wish to pray, But
"Write to us, we will pray for you"
Such invitations lead us into temptations
I always asked somebody to pray for me
I even sent money for prayer warriors
This belittled my confidence in God
Am I right in asking others to pray?

God says:

**No, you are not right
You are all my children
I listen to your prayer
Than others praying for you
If you believe in me, you will surely pray
You seem to believe others than me
If you pray
Your relationship with me will enhance
I know your needs, I know your will
But you should know my will for you
Nobody else can interpret my will for you
Be connected to me, to understand my will**

Thank you Lord, henceforth
I will be in tune with you always....   Amen

2. BIRTHDAY PRAYER

You breathed your breath into me, my God
Made me a human being in your likeness

Today as I remember my birthday
My heart echoes your image in me
You gave mother's womb as my first house
And a beautiful family to take care of me

I owe my heart-felt thanksgiving to you
Wonder whether I deserve all these luxuries
On this birthday I seek your intervention in my life
Correct my understanding of your mission
Check whether I am doing justice to your image in me

Help me save your image in me
Fill my heart with gratitude to you
For holding my hand and leading me
For the lessons that I have learnt so far
For making me realize how unique I am

Bless my parents for their sacrifices for me
Bless my friends for their unreserved friendship
Bless the Church as she presents your love to me
Bless the flora and fauna which nourishes me
Bless this New Year for me

Let me become a new creation in you.. Amen

3. PARENTS PRAYER FOR BIRTHDAY CHILD

We remember with gratitude
Your gift of this child to us
We thank you, O God, the creator
For the marvelous way you shaped this child

Brought a great joy in our lives
Brought a message from you
Brought your love for us
Brought our responsibility to our mind

On this birthday of our child
We remember the gift of parenthood you gave us
And additional responsibilities and wisdom
Help us celebrate this gift in an appropriate way

Let the child realize the values of your kingdom
Let the child grow in your love
Let this child's dreams come true with your help
May all children be good citizens of your kingdom

Equip the child to comprehend your purposes
Enable the child to get proper care and training
Let our sacrifices mould our children's character
Guard them so that they will not go astray

We, the parents and family members
Renew our commitment towards our children. Amen

4. YOUNG GIRL'S PRAYER

Our parent God,
Many times I wonder
Your purpose of creating us
May be you did not expect
When you hear our cries
Being humiliated everywhere
You may be regretting for creating us

Though proud of being the crown of creation
Though happy to know being a female in your image
Though glad to know Mother Mary being your mother
Our happiness seems to be very transitory

Being tortured by men everywhere
Being exposed by media in a bad taste
Being made susceptible for money and popularity tactics
And fallen under vicious circle, forgive us Lord, we
plead

Who will wipe our tears?
Who will restore our dignity?
Won't you teach men to respect us?
Who will save us from all temptations?

Do envelope women with the wings of your love and protection
Our Father God and Mother God... Amen

5. YOUNG MAN'S PRAYER

My young Jesus,
You alone are our model
Proud being young and male
Endowed with dynamism and freedom
Openness and versatile in character

Teach me how to grapple with this world
Parents have their own dreams for me
I have my own dreams which seem to make sense
Depressed being unable to cope with the dreams
Teach me how to go about it

Many ideologies are surrounding us to trap us
Many perished being enslaved to the evil influences
Films add fuel to the fire, misleading the youth with violence
I come to you O Lord Jesus, before I become a prey to evil

Keep us away from terrorist activities
Help us realize that we are needed for the down trodden
Help us realize all human beings are your people
Teach us how to live in this world with your purpose in mind

Please touch our lives
Transform us in order to lead fuller human life
Enliven us in order to live for others
Let youth be torch bearers of your life and peace to Others....   Amen

6. COUPLES PRAYER AT THEIR WEDDING

Thank you Lord,
You have revealed your will for us
And united us in Holy Matrimony
For a life-long companionship

It's our prayer today that
Neither money nor anything else comes in our way
None of us dominate over each other
Help us respect and care for each other

A new relationship has dawned on us
Within us and with our in-laws and neighbors
And through this a greater relationship with you
Help us abide in you, so that we abide in others

On being blessed by parenthood
Equip us to nurture children in your way
Give us wisdom to answer their queries
Empower us to empower children with your values

Let our married life be consecrated for you
Implant in us trust, love and forgiveness
Give us a sense of living for each other
So that we bear witness to your love for us

As we begin our journey of married life
Let your hand hold us and guide us
Make our married life a blessing to us and others.
Amen

7. PATIENTS PRAYER AT THE TIME OF SICKNESS

Lord Jesus, the Physician of physicians
I never blame you for my sickness
It's my own negligence
Forgive my negligence and heal me

Let me not be over anxious about food
Let me be conscious of body up-keep
Let me be mindful about environment
Let me promote health and hygiene

Do teach me to remove all that causes sickness.
Anger, revenge, jealousy, selfishness and others
Do teach me to inculcate good habits
So that I maintain a balanced life

Thank you Lord, for the wisdom you gave doctors
For the medical research and medicines useful to people
For the nursing fraternity whose care is so amazing
For the hospitals which are committed to serve
people

Thank you Lord for people who donate their blood and
eyes
Thank you Lord for people who donate their kidney
Thank you Lord for the facility of transplantation
Thank you Lord, for you have come to us as healer,
heal us now. Amen

8. PRAYER FOR THE SICK

Lord Jesus,
Here is your child on the sick bed
You know the cause of sickness
We know you wish to heal this person
Endow this person with simple trust
in you
Help the doctors to diagnose properly
Let this person extend all the co-
operation
Let the medical staff be kind to the
patient
Embrace this person with healing
wings
Surround this bed with your presence
Let this person experience your compassion and care
Give your wisdom to all those who attend the sick
We join with everybody in prayer to give this person
A quick recovery from the sickness
So that this person resumes his work and leads a normal life
Bless the medicines and food being given to the sick
Bless the nurses, doctors and others attendants
Le your angels guard this person
Enhance in him a complete hope in you
Let this person know that you care for him
And you will heal him as per your terms
Fill this person with thanksgiving for you.
Amen

9. PRAYER BEFORE EXAMINATIONS

Every year at this time
I am traumatized with exam fever
More than me, my parents
Guide us O God to overcome this fever

I am exhausted with competition
Forced on me by parents and teachers
Since exams are merely a memory test
Bestow upon me good memory power

How I wish my body would work like a computer
With keyboard keys set in our body
Soft wear of all subjects fed in
And our hands like a mouse

Due to excess tension
I seem to get fatigued and sick
Many cups of coffee, doses of medicine and junk food
Go in vain; implant in me a spirit of learning, O God

Bless the evaluators not to commit any blunders
Let not university computers do any mistakes
Enable me realize that both prayers and hard work go
together
Prayer answering God, give me good results
Amen

10. PRAYER BEFORE TRAVEL

As I embark on a journey
Into the deep secrets of your creation
Enable me to enjoy the journey
Looking forward to reach the destination safely

Thank you for all the technology which helps our journey
Airplanes, Buses, trains and ships and other means of transportation
And pilots, drivers and navigators
As we meet strangers on the way, help us to see you in them

As we cross tunnels and bridges
Variety of landscapes and waterfalls awaken us to admire your wonderful creation
And keep praising you for this wonderful journey

When we land in a strange place
You kept somebody there to welcome us
A beautiful exposure to other culture with a difference
How blessed are we to be citizens of the world.

How privileged are we to cross several barriers
Keep us alive to the plurality and unity of all people
As pilgrims on this earth and as your children
Keep us engrossed in the beauty of your creation...
Amen

11. PRAYER FOR A NEW HOUSE

Lord of Shelter and all relationships
You are the Lord of our new house
You made this house possible for us
With grateful hearts we praise you

When we were in need of a place,
you showed us the land
When we wanted to build a house, you showed right
plans

When we needed finances, you have opened your
treasury doors

At the time of construction you gave safety to all workers
When the workers needed guidance and wisdom
You gave needed engineers and architects
By your grace alone we could see this house in a
beautiful shape

We thank you Lord for sanctifying this house with
your presence

Thank you Lord for using this place as your dwelling
place

Let all those who live here experience your grace
always

Let this house be a prayer house for all

Help us experience your love and your forgiveness
always ….. Amen

12. OUR PET PLANTS AT HOME

Thank you madam say, the plants
For you feed us with water and manure
In return we give bouquet of flowers
Thank you for treating as living beings

After three days of family outing
Hi , madam where were you all these days?
Don't you know that we depend on you for our survival?
See how lifeless we became without water for three days,
Further delay would have seen us dead and gone
See my neighbor she already lost her life
Now, your tears will not help us grow
Please feed us immediately, we are very hungry
Never forsake us like this any more

Can you stay without food one day?
We too are in need of food every day
 It's God's order for you to take care of us
 We love you as long as you take care of us
 We wish to be ever green to make you ever happy
 We are colorful to make you colorful
The ball is in your court

13. PRAYER FOR THE RESPONSIBILITIES

Lord who am I to be chosen by you?
God says,
You may be weak without any credentials
Just obey me I will use you for my work

Yes Lord here am I, Let it be as per your wish

Remember you are created in my own likeness
Let your love be unbiased, as you represent me(God)
Judge not others without judging yourself
Be a model leader and a human being for others
None of us are perfect, don't be self-righteous
Seek me for guidance and wisdom
Let me be glad for selecting you
Let me not regret for giving you this responsibility

Yes, Lord I was nothing yesterday, today you made me something
I always cherish your call and your confidence in me
I cannot work without seeking your guidance and wisdom
Let me not have any hidden agenda as I accomplish your will
Your will alone should be my will
I will live up to your expectations, and be a blessing to others
Lead me your servant with your compassion…..Amen.

14. MOTHER-IN-LAW'S PRAYER

Lord Jesus,
I dislike this title 'mother in-law'
Since it has a negative connotation
I like to be a mother to my in-laws

Traditionally we are labeled as very cruel and biased
Not all mothers- in-law go along with this trend
Unfortunately our daughters- in-law suspect us
Change our attitudes to one another

As mothers we are so sweet and so sacrificing
We are suddenly changed as daughter- in-law comes
home
We either become terrorists or look like terrorists
After all, daughter in-law comes to be a part of our
family

Some of us have tendency to become very cruel
Since we experienced same treatment in the past
We can't afford to have same tendency in these days
Lord change our attitudes to love our daughters- in-
law

Our in-laws need security, freedom and love
Which they have enjoyed in their mother's house
Help us create a good atmosphere in our home
Help me to continue to be a mother eternally
And accept my daughter in- law as my daughter.
Amen

15. PRAYER FOR OLD AGED PARENTS

Lord Almighty, you have respected the elderly
you remembered your mother even suffering on the
Cross

Our old aged parents are weak, sick and lonely
All that they need at this time
Not our money, not even any luxuries
But our love, our care and our listening to them

Elderly parents left in Old people's home
They gave their life for us, they still love us
It's a great blessing to keep our parents in our home
Lord, help our youngsters to respect the parents

My father and mother who brought me up to this status
Their blessings and hard work put me on right tracks
Should I forget them so soon?
Help me to be grateful to them always

Lord Jesus, help me to respond to their love
Help me to spend quality time with them
Let me take care of their health
Let me be faithful to our parents till their life's end

Lord Jesus Bless our parents
Heal their sickness and loneliness
Help us to continue to love them
And respect them.   Amen

16. PREACHER'S PRAYER

My Master (Guru), you have called me
From the bottom of the society to be your ambassador
How blessed am I to represent you to your people
Without your support I cannot put one step forward

Almost every minute of my life
I am involved in taking decisions
Let me not take decisions to please people
But to please you alone and always

Temptations are always surrounding me
Without being surrendered to temptations,
let me cling to you only
Help me not to compromise with evil, come what may
Lead me lead others in the right path

Equip my faith in order to strengthen the faith of others
Empower me with your spirit to showcase you
through my life
Engage me in your work to live up to your
Gospel demands
Engrave in me your love which can transcend barriers

When I go through rough times in the ministry
Let your Cross comfort me,
When people bully me for their sake
Pardon them and transform them for your sake
Lead me, teach me and envelope me with your spirit.
Amen

17. CONGREGATION'S PRAYER FOR THE PASTOR

Lord Jesus, our High Priest, you have ordained
Our pastor for your ministry among your people
Yes, we see you in our pastor as he represents you for us
He is a gift to us and we are a gift to him

When the pastor breaks the bread for us
We see your image in the pastor
When the pastor exhorts us
We hear you speaking to us

Although the pastor is consecrated for your ministry
Pastor is a human being with all limitations
Help us to be touched by the positive side of the pastor
And the negative side of the pastor, we leave it your
care

We pray for our pastor's health and his family
We beseech you to bless the pastor with your wisdom
We assure our co-operation to the pastor
Bless our ministry together for your sake

No pastor can satisfy all members
As our Lord Jesus also faced opposition
Disgruntled people are everywhere
Empower the pastor with spiritual wisdom
Help us go forward in faith and enjoy your ministry.
Amen

18. PRAYER FOR PEACE

Prince of Peace, Lord Jesus,
Thank you for calling as disciples for peace
As the plurality coupled with violence is increasing
day by day
Inspire us to join you in your struggle to bring peace

You do not desire peace through gun or war
No terrorist can bring peace
Transform the terrorists into lovers of humanity
Enable us to have dialogue with them to bring peace

Enable all communities to believe in peace
Empower all leaders to promote peace
Engage all people in dialogue for peace
Enliven us to peaceful peace process

Transcend barriers of communal feelings
Transform our narrow ideologies and thinking
Transpose our enmity into friendship
Transmit your love for peace in all people

Remove selfish and violent ideologies from us
Remind us that all people are in your own image
Redeem us from being salves to anti-human activities.
Let the will of Prince of Peace prevail. Amen

19. PRAYER FOR THE LEADERS

Lord Jesus, Leader of Leaders
People repose their confidence in their leaders
But leaders don't care for people after they
get their power
Leaders are so bothered about their own security

Who will give security and welfare to ordinary people?
Thank you Lord, still there are some good leaders
Without any inhibitions leaders go to people to serve
them

In fear, innocent people seem to worship some
criminal leaders
Such criminal leaders take the people for a ride
Alluring them with good food and a bottle of cheap liquor
May this land see criminal leaders being transformed?

Let every leader realize that they are chosen
by you, O God
Help the leaders not to help themselves but
to help the poor
Inscribe in them a sense of service
Instill in them your compassion and care
Induce in them a sense of responsibility
Initiate in them taking initiatives to promote life in
others

We live in the midst of multifarious problems
Our leaders need wisdom, patience and your guidance
Provide them a sense of right direction to serve
the people
Let our land experience your reign through these leaders
Amen

20. PRAYER FOR THE CHURCH

Lord Jesus, the founder of the church
Your blood and sacrifice is the foundation
Keep on reminding us about the blood of the martyrs
Let every congregation be reminded of this truth.

If God asks, 'where are you church'?
What should be the answer of the church?
'I am buried under denominational divisions'
'I lost my image through church politics'

We are too happy to indulge in 'happy-clappy' worship services
Holy Communion seem to be the opium, a fear remover
And dolling out few coins in the offertory bag
This seems to be the end of Christianity keeping
Jesus outside the church

Our words are louder than our actions
Our life seem to be contradicting our faith
We need to be a replica of Jesus Christ
We should be talking about Kingdom of
God than hell and satan
May the church become a witnessing community
May the church become a sharing community
May the church become a uniting community
May your Church be practicing your values   Amen

21. PRAYER FOR THE POOR AND DALITS

Lord Jesus, You entered this world as a poor person
Being born in a manager without proper shelter
What an expression of solidarity you showed to the poor

In this caste ridden society
I am labeled as dalit (untouchable)
This label makes me eligible to do only menial works
I am forced to live as non-human being

Lord, are you responsible for our situation today?
Wouldn't you stop this discrimination against us?
Why should we suffer this inferiority complex?
How long should we suffer this ostercization?

Empower those who are sincerely fighting for our liberation
Enroll several agencies to work for our up-liftment
Enable the rich to share their resources with us
Elevate us to live with dignity and integrity

Let not globalization enhance the discrimination
Let not communal forces dominate us
Let not leaders and agencies thrive on our label
Let Dalit leaders be sincere to our cause
Thank you Lord for your presence with us, as God of the poor

Messiah, You alone can save us.   Amen

22. PRAYER AT THE TIME OF BEREAVEMENT

Resurrected Lord Jesus Christ,
We know you
As the Lord of life
Not as the Lord of death
But as the Lord of resurrection

We can reason out this person's death
We can never blame you for the death
You are a life- giver and not a life- taker
We know you are with us helplessly
Shedding tears along with the bereaved family
Your comforting presence wipes our tears

Mortal remains of this person
Remind us of this person's faith and life
A tribute worth emulating words and deeds of deceased
Keep the family and friends in your faith and hope
As we bid good-bye to the deceased
We have learnt lessons from the life of the deceased
We await our time to join you
Let the soul of this person rest in peace   Amen

23. PRAYER AT THE BEGINNING OF A JOB

God of my life, I am delighted to get this job
To earn my livelihood and to help the family
I express my deepest gratitude from the
bottom of my heart
Help me how to do justice to the job I am given

Your help for my studies is unforgettable
You are ever praised for giving me this job
As I enter into this job let me be a learner and doer
Instill in me a commitment and joy to serve your
people

When I am back home
Let me recapitulate the days work
And correct the mistakes I did
And unlearn the prejudices I had

Enthuse me to have a great interest in the job
Infuse in me the job- satisfaction
Enable me not just work for earning the money
But inspire me to fulfill my vocation and your call.

Lord Jesus, give me good health and sound mind
Let my work and attitudes reflect your love for people
Protect me from all dangers and evil influences
Enfranchise me to do justice to the work
And be a great disciple of you through this job…
Amen

24. PRAYER FOR FOOD

God of our life, you provide us the food we need
We thank you immensely for the food we get

Help us to eat without any murmurs
As some people can't even afford to have this

Some of us eat to the needs of our body
Some of us eat to satisfy the taste buds

Not many of us know the pain people go through
Before the food comes on to the table

Struggles of the farmer who produces paddy and
others
Tension, the farmer has to go through for timely rain
and market

Some of us have the choice of food
Even insulting those who prepared the food

Some of us thank God for whatever is placed before us
Enjoy the food with high sense of gratitude to God

Some of us waste food and throw it in dust bins
Not knowing that we are insulting God

When we see some people picking up food
from dust bins
Make us sensitive to hunger of the poor
and needy

Lord, help us respect the food in gratitude to you
Bless the food that is set before us
Being nourished by the food we work and live for
you. Amen

25. PRAYER FOR WATER

Lord of Living waters,
While going through the excruciating pain
You yelled out for water to quench your thirst
Your thirst was not satisfied
Even today thousands of people
Can not afford to get potable water
Many water-borne illnesses are surrounding us
Water is being commercialised and politicised
Our lands are dry, bore wells are dry
Farmers are dying without water resources
Children are dying malnourished
Prices are soaring higher and higher
Diseases are spreading like wild fire
Have mercy upon us and provide us water resources.

Let our lands once again blossom
Let every person have enough resources for survival
Let the leaders understand the needs of people
Let the leaders not be egoistic in their attitudes
Let every person's thirst for water be quenched
Thank you Lord for the showers of rain
O God, bless our land with plenty of water... Amen

26. UNPLUGGED YOU AND GOD

Un-cooperative though I am
Undeniable is your compassion

Under estimated your forgiveness
Undisputed is your concern for us

Unfathomable is your brain
Unequivocal is your creativity

Unexpected are your blessings for us
Unfaithful though are we

Unforgivable are our sins
Unbelievable is your love for sinner

Unintentional are our attitudes
Unlimited is your grace

Unlawful are our daily decisions
Unprecedented are your warnings

Unproductive our works may be
Unceasing your help for us

Uncompromising faith, give me Lord
Unconditional love pour into me

Undoubtedly God, you and me
Unplugged eternally, thank you...Amen

27. INTUITION

Illuminate our lives, O Lord
Impasse be removed from us

Impeccable is your wisdom
Immaturity is the sign of our knowledge

Ill-mannered character be removed from us
Imprint in us your character

Improvise our devotion towards you
Incessant love create in us

Intervene in us through your reign
Intensify your thought pattern in us

Incomprehensible are your works
Indispensible are they for our life

Indoctrinate us with your wisdom
Induce in us our adherence to you

Inestimable are your values
Inevitable for us to cherish and live them

Inexpressible your care for us
Immortalise our life in you

Ingratitude be removed from us
Inscribe in our hearts O Lord eternal gratitude to
you.. Amen

28. PRAYER FOR UNDER-PRIVILEGED CHILDREN

A baby enters into this world with a loud cry
And the people around yell with shouts of joy

Now the child is growing up
He is crying for food and shelter
Lot of food is thrown in the dust bins
What a strange contradiction in our society

As you go to hotels and garages
A tender looking child is at your service
That child is a bread-winner for the family
Tears roll down seeing pathetic situation of that
child

Lord, open the eyes of the rich
Let the society be awakened to redeem such children
Let the children get due respect and enjoy their child-
hood
Let us not have blind eyes and deaf ears to children

Lord Jesus, your intervention is urgently required
To save these deprived children,
Let the children have their share of their childhood joys
You love children and help us to have same love
towards all children
Lord help us to save street children, child laborers,
abused children,
 Mentally and physically challenged children
And all other underprivileged children.   Amen

29. PRAYER FOR WOMEN

Our Creator God
Woman was created as the crown of creation
We kept them into the depths of degradation
A woman cries,

Lord you blessed my marriage, its not going on well
Day and night I am being tortured by my husband
and in-laws
I can neither leave the family nor live alone
The only way to escape the torture is suicide
Which I feel is against your will for me.
There are so many women like me suffering

Why are you so silent on us O Lord?
Did you create us to suffer in the world?
You came to give us fuller life, aren't you?
Do you want us to depend on you or not?
Are you blind and deaf for our cries?
Do you want us to take the law into our hands?

Transform men who torture women
Let our in-laws treat us as their own kith and kin
Awaken the church, society and leaders to bring
Justice, safety and protection and dignity to all women
Let your love surround women to protect them and
give them full life.. Amen

30. FORGIVE TO BE FORGIVEN

Forgiving Lord,
Whenever we look at a person
Who committed a small mistake, our hearts rejoice
Not realizing that we are hiding our mistakes within

My dear forgiving God, I do not know how I fell for that sin
I realized my mistake and I beseech you to forgive me
I am very sure I have received your pardon and new life

But my church has not forgiven me, as if they have not committed any sin
They do not allow me to lead a normal life and look at me as a criminal
Now I pray that you forgive these people who do not forgive others
Let them understand they are in the ministry of reconciliation

None of us are perfect and live as hypocrites
Every Sunday we confess our sins and seek forgiveness
Still we have superiority complex over other people
Let there not be a breach of relationship within the church

Lord Jesus, you have asked us to forgive to receive your forgiveness
Give us a tolerant mind to forget and forgive the sins of others
As you have forgiven them already, help us to accept your forgiveness
You always see good in us whereas we see bad in others
Forgive us our sins, enable us to see others as you see them. Amen

31. THE CREATOR OF HELL AND SATAN?

Creator God, in the beginning
You saw everything you created was good
Soon you felt sorry for your own creation
You destroyed the whole creation through flood
And recreated everything through Noah

In both occasions
Thank you for not creating hell
And also the so-called Satan
Yes, we the human beings brought evil

Our preachers enjoy preaching Satan and hell
In fact they flourish by threatening the innocent
They preach very less about you and your compassion
Teach them Hell and Satan are non-existent

Knowing you as our Father and Mother and
forgiving God
How can we expect you to create hell and
send us there?
We suffer punishment for every mistake
committed here only
We are your children and we come back to you
You have defeated all evil forces and concepts

Through your Cross and Resurrection
You even said kingdom of God/Heaven is in you
Thank you Lord, help us to live in you ever and ever
Amen

32. THE CREATED AND THE CREATOR

Given a chance, your created beings
Would attempt a narco -analysis test on your brain
To find out amazing factors about your brain
Since your brain is behind beautiful creation around us

How graceful and beautiful are your handiworks
When tender breeze touches us;
When lovely colors appear in the sky;
When plants and trees blossom in their time
When birds fly high in the sky
We simply admire your works and salute you

Our anatomy showcases your brilliance;
The working pattern of our brain and nerves
The flow of blood, water and air in our body
The role of pancreas, kidney and liver and other parts of
the body
More amazing is the way our heart functions non-stop
And the unity of all members of body is astounding

Change of seasons remind us your care for us
Floods and Tsunami points out our greed
Sickness and suffering point out our negligence
Enable us, O God, to be good stewards of your creation
So that generations to come would benefit from your
handiwork.. Amen

33. CAN YOU CONVERT ME?

Who are you to convert me?
Is it necessary for me to get converted?

Yes Lord, do I have required credentials
to ask others to get converted to my religion?
When I compare my life-style with others life- style
many of us feel we are not true to our Lord Jesus
Christ

Without being changed we ask others to change
'Judge not' our Lord said, we seem to say 'why not'?
we should judge our selves before we judge others
let us accept 'change' before we ask others to change

We need to be converted from self-righteousness
We need to be converted from false prestige
We need to be converted from selfish attitudes
We need to be converted from 'dominating others'

Let us remember that it is God who converts
Not you and me or any evangelists
We need to cooperate with God for
Such transformation
converting for better life is divine and personal
Nobody can stop converting people for good life.
Amen

34. PRAYER ON SUNDAY

'Holy day' has been converted by some as 'holiday'
People wish to earn more money then better life
There are some who forego earnings on Sunday to attend
worship
Lord Jesus, let people experience your grace anew in
the worship

God almighty, we are sorry, you
have respected us so much
In turn we are insulting you by
ignoring Sunday worship
Yet, you tolerate us and forgive
us to realize our mistakes
Enable your people to realize the
value of Community worship

As I come to your sanctuary with my family
We are so much lifted up in worshiping you
When we sing together, pray together,
Partake in the Holy Communion, fellowship outside
the church
We experience nothing but your love and your grace
Once in a week we are delighted to meet one another
To exchange greetings and strengthen our bonds of love
Your love and your grace is sufficient for you
Thank you Lord for giving us this unique worship service
Let the Sunday worship be a wake up call for our life
 Help me and my family never to miss Sunday blessings
Help us to enrich one another through this worship
Help us to get connected to you through this worship…
Amen

35. PRAYER FOR PRIORITIES

As I wake up along with the prayers of the birds
Songs of praise by various religions and the rising of the
sun
My hearts jumps with joy for getting another exciting
day
Many agendas comes to mind with many motives
Many times I miss the direction due to wrong priorities
At the dawn every day I seek your guidance for the day

Lord, how should I spend the day?
How should I spend the money I have?
What should be my priorities?
Whom should I satisfy, boss, wife, parents, myself or
you?

How do I understand your will for me for this day?
Lord, open my eyes to read in between the lines
Open my ears to listen to your voice and accordingly
Open my heart not to entertain any hidden agenda
Open my minds to comprehend your will for me

Empower me with right priorities
Enable me to experience your presence
As you lived for others with right priorities
Help me to live for others who are your children
Amen

36. PRAYER FOR THE PET DOG

What a paradoxical situation, O Lord
We cannot live with our own siblings happily
But we are so happy and fond of our pet dogs
They have become wonderful companions for us

'Justy' is the name of our pet dog, a
very faithful creature
Thank you for keeping 'Justy' with us for sometime
We had to keep him in the church compound
Hoping that we would move there very soon
That dream did not come to a reality
Very soon 'Justy' came to know the members
of the church
Church members used to love him very much
He did not spare any other person coming
into the church

The news of 'some dogs bit Justy and killed him'
was shocking to us
We rushed to the church to give a tearful funeral
Tears just roll down like any thing after seeing
'Justy' in that situation
We bid good-bye to Justy and buried him in the
church compound

We do not know what to pray at this time
We pray that you would kindly console us
Help people to experience your love through
such pet animals
It's a great feeling that human beings and
animals can live together
Give us same sense of love towards each other… Amen

37. PRAYER FOR THE ENVIRONMENT

Engrossed by the elegance of your creation
Entitle me to become poetic gazing at the
splendor of moon and stars
Enfold me in ecstatic position in the
sunrise and sunset
Engage me in an attitude of exaltation in April showers

We are sorry Lord; we are desecrating your creation
Not realizing that we need to be stewards
of your creation

Not many realize that we are living by your creation
Trees shed tears when some one put an axe on them

The trees are telling us, 'Sorry we cannot help anymore'
'I am dead and gone' other trees are mourning, you may
not know

How can we save ourselves from impending disaster?
How can we leave a decent atmosphere for
future generation?

As we experience the extinction of certain birds
and animals
Should we not feel indisposed and insulted for
this act of cruelty?

Lord, teach us to take care of our environment
Open our senses to the cruelty meted out to the environment

Endue us with right attitude towards nature
Enliven us to the realities of environment to our life
Enrapture us to experience your image in nature
Entrust us to eradicate violence on nature.   Amen

38. PRAYER FOR THE SOLDIERS

We are extremely sorry, Almighty God
Very rarely we remember soldiers in our prayers
Although they are working day and night
Defending and protecting the sovereignty of our
country

As the soldiers tread valleys and mountains and forests
To guard our country, they need your protection O Lord
Let each soldier be strengthened by the Psalm
'Even though I walk through the valley and shadow of
death I fear no evil' for God is with me sung by King
David

We pray for the families who have lost their bread winner
We pray for those soldiers who are at the border
Fighting our cause
We praise you for their courage and commitment
and sacrifice
We pray that you would empower them with alertness
and wisdom

Lord, not only our country save all other countries
Both from foreign and local terrorists
Lord, save the world from wars and violent plans
Whenever these people involve in killing people
Let them realize that they are killing you O God

Save us also from nuclear threat and other
dangerous weapons
O Lord, let all the soldiers experience your
loving protection
Help them to have a very satisfied and
wonderful life…Amen

39. PRAYER FOR HOSPITALS AND MEDICAL FRATERNITY

The second temple for all us are hospitals
And the next to God are our doctors and nurses
Doctor of Doctors Lord Jesus Christ,
What a brilliant mind you gave to medical fraternity
They repair our body and restore our life from sickness
We honestly admire the advancement in
medical sciences
They are to be venerated for their services rendered
They generally do not have any discrimination
against anybody
Wish people around the world would imitate the
medical community

We continue to pray that the medical fraternity will
continue as service people not as commercial exploits
Let drug producers not adulterate the drugs
Provide hospitals enough infrastructures to treat
patients

Bless all those who take care of people and give them
tolerance
Bless all the management boards and administrative
staff
Bless all the paramedical staff and maintenance staff
Bless all involved in healing ministry that they represent
God for us..Amen

40. PRAYER FOR JUSTICE

Lord of Justice,
Your people are living in the midst of injustice
Let the leaders, lawyers, judges, politician and
religious heads deliver justice to people without
any bias on caste and creed
Empower your leaders and others not to
become slaves of corruption

Millions of people are crying for justice
Thousands of people are languishing in prisons
without trial and suffering injustice
Cannot afford to have lawyers to fight their case
Many children are dying due to adulterated medicines
and food
Many women and young girls are being exploited
Crimes are increasing day by day
Innumerable cases are pending in courts for judg-
ment

Lord, intervene in our society to enable us to see
a just society
Lord, Let the world know that we are under your
reign and justice
Certainly you are not in favor of anarchy and injustice
Definitely you want us to live in peace and justice.
Let your reign, bring justice and peace
Let your reign prevail among us and give us a
decent life. Amen

41. MUSICAL MIND OF GOD

Lord of melody and rhythm
Wah, what a musical mind you have
Bless you God for the gift of music for us
Music enthralls our being and brings healing to us
Melody moves into our system so spontaneously
Rhythm moves our body into dancing postures
Tuned words keep us in celestial mood
Harmony of voices bring harmony to our body

How blessed are our bodies to respond to musical beats
How privileged are we to sing and to listen to songs
Music indeed transports into a divine world
Music awakens the lazy and the sick to life

As we hear spiritual songs of all religions
Our hearts jumps up with a thrilling joy
Thank you Lord for rejuvenating our life through music
Thank you Lord for entering into us
Through music
Let music spring in us a deep love for you
Sustain us and enliven us with your creativity.   Amen

42. PRAYER FOR MOTHERS

Our life in our mother's womb which you created
Cannot be described with any stretch of imagination
We simply adore you for creating a mother

We come out with tears in our eyes and crying
For the pain mother had to go through for nine months
To make me a citizen of this world
It was both a farewell and welcome time
A lovely smile comes on in the face of the proud
mother
All well wishers join me in celebration
And a new title bestowed upon her 'Mother'

Sleepless nights and restless days are symbolic of a
mother
Sacrifice is another name for Mother next to God

Mother's compassionate touch
Mother's soothing words, Mother's unreserved love
Mother's caring warmth

Has supernatural and divine feeling for any child
Unfortunately many children forget mothers very soon
We beseech you to bless all mothers in the world
For, they are your representatives for us.   Amen

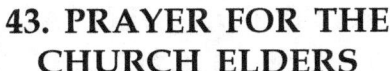

43. PRAYER FOR THE CHURCH ELDERS

As you were the Guru for your disciples, O God
Let the church pastor reflect you for the elders
as their Guru
May the church elders be like disciples and not
as Pharisees
Elders should consider themselves as gifted
Servants of our Lord

Church elders come from different walks of life
With different talents and different schools of thought
Church elects them to assist in pastoral ministry
They do sacrifice lot of money and time for the church

Lord, help the elders to assist the pastor with the wisdom
from above
Help the pastor to guide the leaders as the shepherd leads
the sheep

Enable the elders to follow Jesus Christ in their work
No secular administration should dominate the church life

Help the elders and the pastors not to succumb to petty
politics
Help them to please God alone and not any other person

Let the ministry of reconciliation be focused
Let them all work united for the spiritual growth
Let all the elders and pastor keep in their mind
That every person in the church belongs to God's family

Enable the elders and pastors to follow the values of the cros
Taught by our Lord Jesus Christ and set an example. Amen

44. PRAYER FOR MENTALLY AND PHYSICALLY CHALLENGED

Lord of all Children,
Every mother wants to know
Why this child is born with defects?
What should be our answer to them?

Certainly it's not a curse from you
It's because of certain biological irregularities
Help the parents to love the child as precious
Since every child born in the world is precious to God

Their love towards this child should be more than the normal children
Certainly each of them posses some great talents
Thank you Lord for those who are working for them
to bring out best in them
We admire their commitment and care

Enable the society to have compassion on such children
Let the teachers and institutions be strengthened to serve them better
Let the parents of such children give special care for them
Let all the religious institutions provide special budget for them
May the Good Lord help these children to challenge the society
May these children make a great contribution to the society
Let mentally and physically challenged children have a great life.   Amen

45. THE HOLY SPIRIT

The Holy Spirit is with us
Why call 'come Holy Spirit'?
He is not somewhere up above
He has come to stay with us
We need to open our minds and hearts
Call ourselves to come to the presence of the Holy
Spirit

Yes, some shout loudly ordering the spirit to come
And they even order the Spirit to get out with a bell
Sorry, they are yet to experience the presence of God
Holy Spirit is no other than God or Christ being
present with us

Yes, Holy Spirit/Christ/God is working is us
Renewing us, reforming us, rejuvenating us
and even guiding us
The Holy Spirit is our counselor, guide and a friend
 Believe and enjoy God being with us all the time

Our Lord Jesus Christ was filled with God's spirit
 But never jumped, clapped and danced and shouted
Not even spoken languages not known to any body
He was serving the humanity with God's power

Hereafter to us not call or order him to come down
Shout and invite yourself to the presence of Holy Spirit
with us
So that you will have a fulfilling and amazing life in God.

46. PRAYER FOR FAMILIES

Parent of all the families on this earth
Your creative mind has created 'family'
Our selfish nature breaking down the families
Thus bringing destruction to your created world

Help us to realize that we are all members of your family
What a precious gift you have given to us for our
survival

The unity that exists in the family
The security that we have in the family
The love that we share in the family
The respect we have for one another
Incomparable to any institution
It's an amazing grace from God
Nothing should divide us,
Either money or status
Either selfishness or pride
Either relatives or neighbors

Lord Jesus, you are the head of the family
Control our emotions and passions
Dispel all the darkness in the family life
Help us to glorify you through our family life. Amen

47. THANKSGIVING FOR THE NEW LEASE OF LIFE

Thank you Lord Jesus
For listening to my prayers
For your care when I was in the sick bed
For creating the healing process
For guiding me to a good doctor
For touching my medicines
For preparing me for treatment
For your presence at the operation table
For nursing care for their healing touch and words
For the dedicated doctors and surgeons
For your comforting presence around my bed
For all my family members and their solidarity
For all the necessary help received from friends
For liberating me from my sickness
For the lessons learnt through this situation
For giving me a new lease of life to witness you

You are my messiah, you are my healer
You are my doctor, you are my protector
You are my Guru, You are my Friend,
You are my creator, you are the Lord Life
Thank you and Thank you for the new lease of life
for me.. Amen

48. PRAYER FOR UNITY

O Trinitarian God, you are one and we belong to that
oneness
We have divided your church into several pieces
On the basis of selfishness, tradition, culture, theology,
nationality, caste, color, language and even personality
cult

Our identity is not Christianity, but the division we
represent Unable to bear witness to you as a divided
church

Remind us once again your prayer for unity of all people
Grant us wisdom to understand your purposes for unity
Help us not to hate each other as we are different
from one another
Open our minds to see and experience the unity in
the Godhood

Help us respect each other and accept each other
All of us bear your image in us and belong to your
family
The divisions are not your expectations
Support us to breakdown the walls of separation

Lord, transform our stubborn and selfish minds
 Heal the wounds that are inflicted
Transform the theology of divisions into theology of
unity
Redeem us from disunity and disintegration
Help us not to crucify you again and again
Guide us to experience unity in diversity
Let the church remain as one family of God… Amen

49. PRAYER FOR TEACHERS

Jesus the Guru (teacher and a Master)
You are with us to dispel the darkness in people
You called teachers to follow your example
Let the teacher's commitment be enhanced

Bless the teachers with your wisdom
Let the students be treated as teacher's own children.
Let them know that they are called for a noble profession
Bequeath upon the teachers your strength and your
humility

Forgive their mistakes of the teachers as they too
are human
Let them answer the queries raised by students politely
Appreciation and care be the teacher's methodology
The weaker children may not be discriminated against

Empower teacher to set an example for their wards
Encourage teachers to teach your values to pupils
Enable them infuse in children a responsibility
towards society
Enthuse in children awareness towards the poor

Thank you Lord for the wonderful teaching fraternity
we have
Thank you Lord for the infrastructure for the children
to enjoy
Thank you for the all round development schools insist
for children
Help the teachers transform the society through
education... Amen

50. HOW WONDERFUL ARE WE!

How wonderfully you have weaved us ,O Creator
And bestowed upon us;

A sense of laughter, a sense to lament
A sense of appreciation to express our feelings
A sense of experiencing your presence with us
A sense to love and forgive
No words can express our gratitude to you for all these.

When I look inside my biological chemistry
Nervous system, bones, flesh, blood, water
Sugar, salt, water, air, energy producing glands
A mind with so much of memory power
A heart with so much of compassion
We are excited to know how wonderfully you shaped us

Sorry, Lord we misused many blessings you gave us
Instead of showing compassion we showed anger and
revenge
Instead of singing your praises we gossiped always
Lord teach us to use our personality to bring glory to
you

Help us to maintain the hardware and software you gave
us
How blessed are the human beings to have your character
in us
Help this wonderful body to reflect your grace and love
May you always be praised through this wonderful life.
Amen

51. LIFE IS A JOURNEY

From the unity of wife and husband
Begins a journey of our life
Life in the embryo is towards becoming
Being to becoming is an on going process
Life is to becoming something
Childhood to old age is a becoming process
A longing to become something is our perennial quest

Every step towards growing is precious
Every direction we go is auspicious
Every person we meet is to be celebrated
Every event we go through is an eye-opener

Every effort we take is part of the journey
Every failure we face to be cherished
Every success we get is to be thanked
Every job undertaken to be performed well

Every village, town, city and the country enthralls us
Drops of rain, heat of the sun, elegance of moon awesome
What a glorious life we have in this world
Let us enjoy the journey with gratitude to God
Mortality to immortality is the next flight

52. GOD

Quest for God has been for ages
It will continue to be an endless search
Philosophers, poets and theologians have dealt exten-
sively
Human beings even christened God with several names

God survives in various forms in various cultures
Yet, God is being insulted by parochial thinking
Violence is increasing in the name of God
Temples, doctrines, rituals are flourishing
Yet, reverence for God's people is at the low ebb

God has been very much domesticated in their own
concepts
People create enmity between each concept of God
For the survival of their God and their religious
profession
Poor God must be with mixed feelings

I found God in Jesus Christ
Mother Teresa found God in every human heart
Some people find God in suffering
Some find God in nature: sun, flowers and so on
Some believe God is in temples, pilgrim centers
I believe God is with us, in full control of the universe
Names and forms of God do not matter, But God matters
Give reverence to God and enjoy the life given to us.

53. CASTE

God is ignored by popular evil called CASTE
Each caste creates its own God
Caste became God
And defended her own rituals and philosophy
In the process human beings are threatened to their life
This caste-ism in this form has been here for a long time
God is not responsible for this evil
All evil comes from human beings alone

I am being looked down by people as an inferior being
Without me they can not survive, but I am like 'use and through'
I am being rebuked badly, beaten badly, my family is being humiliated
I am being treated as bonded laborer for years
I do not even know whether there is any alternative life for me
If there is such life who will offer me life worth living
Caste is undermining the human dignity
Thus belittling God's creation
Those who follow caste are anti-human and anti-God
Caste-ism should not be allowed to prosper by any way
Caste-ism can be eradicated with concerted efforts
Let us join hands to break this sin in India.

54. CORRUPTION

Un-accountable currency is being unearthed
They made themselves rich and others poor
Our land is a rich land with poor sharing
Our leaders have neither ears nor eyes nor heart
Corruption makes the rich richer, the poor the poorer

Corruption has entered in all fields of life
Including religion, education and law departments
Of-course, politicians are the foster-parents of corruption
People are forced to yield to corruption to get things done
It has come to stay that we cannot survive without
corruption.

What do these people do with such enormous money?
How many houses can they build with such money?
How can they get sleep with all the black money?
Don't they have any fear of God for looting other's
livelihood.

O God, I am being tortured by corruption every step I take
O God, you are being murdered by corruption everywhere
O God, do you hear the cries of the innocent people?
O God, Why don't you send somebody to stop this
corruption
O God, You too may be trapped by corruption if you take
any action
People even come to you with bribe for prosperity through
corruption
Save us, O God from corruption, if you can, otherwise
empower us.

55. PRAYER FOR TERRORISTS

Terrorists are human beings with wrong orientation to life
Their leaders take them for a ride to satisfy
their own revenge
Neither terrorist nor their leaders are under
the reign of God
No concept of God encourages killing God's own
creation.

Terrorists and their leaders do not value the
life given by God
Every religion is to spread the love of God to all people
Innocent blood of the victims is haunting the terrorists
Victim's families have been in tears and depression.

Lord God, can you not intervene in the life of the terrorists
to stop their crimes on the innocent people
and their families?

Lord Jesus put an axe on the wrong ideologies
of the leaders who implant in people violence in the
name of God and ideology

God almighty, teach the terrorists the values of life
God, teach who involve in violence the fear of God
God, let no one use your name to promote violence
God, let terrorists surrender to your love and your peace

Jesus, let people listen to your voice and your will
Jesus, let people practice love, peace and justice to all
people
Jesus, let not people live on the blood and pain of others
Jesus, let your kingdom come and your will only be
done. Amen

56. TIME

God's marvelous gift for you and me is Time
Time is more precious a wealth and possessions
One who neglects time neglects ones own life and God
Time keeps on moving, it will never wait for us

Time says,
Come and marry me, I will give you life
Embrace me; I will give warmth to your life
Kiss me; I will make your life to be remembered by all
Carry me with you; I will enhance your life

Time wakes us up from slumber
Time sharpens our life and makes us smart
Time teaches punctuality and patience
Time gives warnings for future life

Time reminds us about God the giver of life and time
Time reminds us of our focus in our life
Time reminds us of our duty-consciousness
Time reminds us of several changes in our life

God of time and God of life, Thank you for life and time
Which you have bestowed upon us to enjoy life through time
Forgive us when we misuse our life and time given to us
Help us to use the time and life as you expected us to do. Amen

57. PRAYER FOR INDIA

Our mother land India is magnificent in every aspect
A beautiful amalgamation of several beautiful cultures
Our land is blessed with people with great hospitality
Our brains are superfine and shining every where

Of late, due to some influences, violence has taken and
upper hand
Political leaders are living for their own ideologies not for
people
Government's work is God's work' is not being practiced
We are rich in resources but poor in sharing equally by all

Outsourcing centers are destroying the ethos of our youth
Techies are suffering with too much pressure in work
Families and the society is being affected with several
problems
People and the government are the at cross roads

In this scenario we come to you O Lord, for your comfort
We seek your intervention in our life with your justice and
peace
We pray for the soldiers, political as well as religious
leaders
Teachers, scientists, medical professionals, factory workers
Let each one us shoulder the responsibility towards our
nation
Let no caste, religion, language, region and ideology divide
us
Empower us to safeguard the beauty of our beautiful land,
India
Let all of us enjoy your rule in this land and all over
the world. Amen

58. FARMER

Food and farmer go hand in glove
Seasonal rains, seeds and support are his assets
Industrialization has diminished the farmer
Lack of rains, seeds and support made his life miserable
Who needs to be blamed ? God or Globalization
The source of life is in doldrums.

Do we realize that the farmer needs to be supported?
Do we realize our mistake in not getting enough rains?
Do we now see the consequences of our misuse of
environment?
Don't we think it is the right time for us to safeguard
the earth?

Lord, teach us how to save this earth for the future
Lord, help us help the farmer who helps us for our
livelihood
Lord, remove the greediness from our dictionaries
Lord, remove the dominance of businessmen on the
Farmer

Thank you Lord, for the hard work the farmer puts in to
feed us
Thank you Lord, for his patience waiting for seasons
and rains
Thank you Lord, for the struggle he goes through to get
seeds
Thank you Lord, for his careful watch over his crops

Bless O my Lord, the farmers and their families
Bless our lands with fertility and rains
Bless of our farmers with good health and necessary
facilities Amen

59. DIALOGUE

I am a Christian, She is a Hindu and he is a Muslim by faith
But by birth we are all human beings in the likeness of God
God lives in all of us and works through all of us
For the welfare of all people irrespective of creed and culture

All of us need God, religion, rituals to lead a reasonable life
Each religion may claim they are superior as they are conditioned
Religions exist to bring all people together and not to divide people
No concept of God would warrant a fatwa against God's created beings

God is one but He exists with variety of names christened by people
We should not divide the God-hood with our own selfish nature
Religion is what we practice and should go for self-examination
The dialogue helps us to discover our strengths and weaknesses

We gather for dialogue not to force our religion on others
But respect each of our religions and learn from one another
Many inter-religious groups around the word are progressing well
To bring peace and dignity to every human person of every religion

Almighty God of all people inspire us to come together
Enable us to learn that we all belong to your family
Let not our religious differences bring disgrace to you,
O God
Let peace and harmony rule our hearts and minds
And our land. Amen

60. PRAYER FOR FRIENDS

Friends are many times useful, some times harmful
Friendship is the greatest relationship God gave us
Friendship is loving each other without any tags attached
Friendship does not mean in narrow sense of love or romance

Friendship does not exist with certain pre-conditions
Friendship does not have any boundaries of creed and culture
Friendship does not grow in doing favors to one another.
Friendship could exist even within family relationships

Friends do not exploit one another for their sake
Friends accept their own weaknesses and strengths
Friends sacrifice their life to enrich one anothers life
Friends fare better than their blood relatives

How blessed are we Jesus, to be invited as your friends
We long to have good friends in our life's journey
Lord, give the privilege to have friendship with you and others
Give us a mind to transform the weaknesses of our friends

Lord Jesus, help us to live for our friends
Help us God, to pray for our friends for their good life
Enable all friends to promote life on this earth
Let your compassion and justice widen the bonds of friendship. Amen.

61. PRAYER FOR
THE LENTEN DAYS

O GOD,
Your incarnation, Jesus Christ, rules the hearts of
millions
 His teachings, values and life echoes around the world
Jesus is the man for celebration and God for salvation
His life is a unique combination of word and deed
No one is so forgiving and so compassionate to people
A challenging life he lived in the midst of orthodoxy of
Judaism
He fought courageously against the hegemony of the
Roman Empire
The world salutes him during this Lenten season
Lord Jesus, How great you were to forgive people who
hurt you
How concerned you were to offer paradise to the
repentant sinner
How responsible you were to take care of your mother
even from the cross
How bold you were to go through that excruciating
pain during those days
What kind of torture you went through for speaking the
truth
For the sake of humanity you did not mind the pain
We are ever grateful to you, My Lord Jesus Christ
On my knees I boldly confess that you are my hero for
ever
Though we feel sorry for your sufferings, we are proud
of you.

Your sufferings have taken away our sufferings
Your life showed us how to lead this human life
How privileged we are to be your disciples, save us
now. Amen

My forgiving God,
I am blind and defend my mistakes
I never realize my mistakes in my life
I behave so self-righteous
Open my blind heart to realize my mistakes.
Amen

Thank you Lord for this season of Lent
To regret for our mistakes of the past and present
We cannot hide from you what we are
Enable me to see the hidden sinner in me. Amen

A season of spring is with us in the form of Lent
Let old and biased leaves fall from us
Renew us with new shoots of leaves in our faith
Give death to our sins and a resurrection to our life.
Amen

In your death on the cross you showed your guts
We are yet to get your courage
You stood there both as representative of people and
God
Experiencing injustice from the earth and love of God
from above
Give us grace to witness the pain of the people and
grace of God. Amen

You took care of your mother and your disciple in the
midst of pain

Very often we ignore the importance of parents in our life
You touched our hearts who neglected our responsibilities
Let our parents receive your grace through us. Amen

Lord Jesus, you brought us home God who sacrifices his life for all of us
In spite of our disobeying you and being disloyal to you
Your compassion overpowers our frailty and empowers our confidence
Transform our brittleness into strong hope in you. Amen

****

Children forsake their parents, friends forsake their friends
But you never forsake us; sorry we have forsaken you at times
We made you cry 'why have you forsaken me O, God'
How horrible it is to have been forsaken by people
Let not even enemies have this kind of horrible feelings. Amen

****

We yield ourselves to sin despite we are in your image
Since we enjoy sin we become weak and sinful
When we practice and enjoy God, we retain the image of God in us
Lord Jesus, enable us to enjoy your image in our life for ever. Amen

****

Resurrected Lord Jesus, reign over us with new lease of life. Amen

62. GOOD FRIDAY PRAYERS
(Children's perspective)

Our dear loving Dad, Jesus Christ
Where did all children go
When you were carrying the cross?
You loved children so much that I wish I was there
To wipe your tears and to protest your carrying the Cross
We ourselves would have carried the Cross.   Amen

Jesus, you are our loving father and mother
Though my parents scold us and punish us
You always loved us
Yes Lord, though you know what they were doing
You have forgiven them, thank you for your forgiveness. Amen

Jesus, what a beautiful paradise you have assured us in you
Than bungalows built by my parents
Help me to experience paradise in you
By accepting my mistakes and seeking your
forgiveness. Amen

My dear Jesus, How nice of you to remember
Your mother and your disciples
To showcase the importance of relationships
Help us O God to respect our mother and father
And others in our neighborhood   Amen
My dear God, How often we, the children
Lonely and uncared for
How often children are seen crying
Being forsaken by mothers
We understand how you would have felt

Being forsaken by your own disciples
You taught us that God will never forsake us. Amen

Dear Jesus, we learnt in our Sunday school
That you are the author of Living waters
But when you were thirsty
There was none to quench your thirst
I wish I was there to give you water
Soldiers would not have allowed me to reach you
I would have reached God to shower rain waters on
you. Amen

Dear Lord Jesus,
How wonderful are your words and deeds
You have beautifully accomplished
What you were assigned to do by God
Give us same guts and confidence to say that
'We will accomplish what God wants us to do.
Amen

Dear Lord Jesus, You proved the world that
Your life was in God's loving hands
You have fulfilled God's will on this earth
How confidently and courageously you have handed
over
Your life into the hands of the creator- God
Help us to have same trust in God. Amen

Thank you Lord for providing us the
Hot cross buns to celebrate your victory on the cross
We await the Easter eggs
To remind ourselves about your resurrection
Thank you Lord Jesus for giving us a new Hope and a
new Life
Help us to promote life on this earth. Amen

63. DEATH

Know I will die one day or the other
But I do not realize when I will breathe last
I also know I will join God the creator
I do not believe in Hell, as God did not create it

I will not be able to cry on my death
Because I begin eternal life through death
People around me will lament over my death
Because still they are on earth languishing in pain

After my death there will be crisis in the family
About my bank account, property, funeral expenses and
so on
And I will be interceding to God for all people

I do not know what assignment I will get in the eternal
life
If I had a choice to choose the assignment
I will accept the work of cleansing the minds of the
leaders
So that at least our children would enjoy a just society
 on this earth
I am not afraid of death, since I know it is inevitable
Till the last minute of my life I wish to reflect Lord Jesus
in my life
I keep thanking God for this beautiful life on this lovely
earth
If this earth itself is so lovely imagine the presence of
God.

64. JESUS CHRIST

People may come and people may go in my life
But Jesus Christ will remain in my heart and mind for ever
He would continue to live in the world transforming people
His compassion and concern for people is so unique
His healing touch is so joyful and so consoling
His teachings are so valuable and so marvelous
His life and teachings have already transformed many lives
Anybody of any culture could easily emulate Jesus Christ.

His Cross is the foundation for my ministry and life
In times of trouble it is the Cross of Christ which healed
me Jesus is not somewhere sitting in heaven
Jesus Christ is present in our midst in the form of the Holy
Spirit
We do not need to call him; we should call ourselves to
him His life is a great model for any human person
His humility and compassion is worth following

For the last two thousand years he has been celebrity in the
world
People would continue to celebrate him even in the million
years to come
Only those who do not realize his presence with us, look
for his second coming
My Lord Jesus is with me, forgiving my mistakes and
leading me
This is the reason that I cannot do anything which brings
disgrace to Jesus
May the Good Lord Jesus Christ live in me and you for
ever.

65. MOTHER TERESA

On March 5th 1995, a memorable day for me
I reached her home to have a glimpse of her
To my luck, she was there and I waited for her
As she walked down the corridor from her office
I could not believe my eyes that was Mother Teresa.

I was delighted and excited to touch her hands
For a minute I was in a trance and forgot myself
As if God had touched me, my joy k new no bounds
The time that I spent with her was the most rewarding time in my life

She is my favorite Christian lady around the world
I am very much inspired by her words and life and work
A woman who loved Jesus Christ with honesty
A Philanthropist to the core who served the poorest of the poor

Whose 'Missionaries of Charity' spread around the world
Made a great bench mark for Jesus and serving the poor
How can I and the world ever forget this great woman of faith?
The hierarchy of the Church need not grant her saint-hood
God has already honored her with saint hood
Long live Mother Teresa in the lives of humanity.

66. GANDHIJI

I had the privilege of visiting Sevagram near Nagpur
Where Gandhiji used to live for some time
Very excited and blessed to see his ashram
Sure he must have spent time here in thinking of India

Father of the nation and hero of the people
Who got us freedom through non-violence
A simple man with great vision and profound thoughts
A great leader for the biggest democracy in the world

Gandhiji has fought with great British Empire peacefully
He was inspired by the Sermon on the Mount by Lord Jesus
He practiced so many Christian values learnt from Jesus
His life and teachings have become a blue print for
many nations

I admire him for his courage and stamina and the focus of
his mission
He was a man who set models of leadership in him
Many places in India and abroad bear his name,

His khadi movement earned a great name in the industry
His movement of non-violence is being practiced around
the world
He needs to be studied and followed, some even worship
him
Gandhiji will live in the lives of the people for ever and
ever.

67. THE SECOND COMING OF JESUS CHRIST

For the last two thousand years since Jesus died and rose
Few Jews did not believe in Jesus Christ as a King to come
For those who accepted Jesus as savior the second
coming is of no consequence
Because Jesus Christ is with us today in the form of the
Holy Spirit
Do we not recognize the presence of God with us? What
else do you want?
Jesus himself said the Kingdom of God is within you.
What else do you expect?
Let us recognize the presence of God and enjoy life in
Christ.

Let us not be threatened by some rumors of so many
things and dates
So many groups of people predicted the dates and
perished for good
We should be happy if our Lord appears again to our
eyes
Let us expect for that great joyous movement on this
earth
Whatever might happen fear not because we are God's
family
If we believe in Jesus Christ you will not worry about
anything

Earth quakes and thunders come due to our misuse of nature

Scientists say there is lot of life for this earth some billion years

Sectarians and others threaten people and inflict fear in them

Nothing to worry, God is with us and going to be with us for ever

Let us whole heartedly recognize the presence of God with us

Let people realize that Jesus Christ is in charge of this world.

Don't worry, be happy, Let us enjoy life in Jesus Christ.

Let us happily receive Christ, if he comes in our time.

68. PRAYER FOR SCIENTISTS

Omnipotent God,
Why did you give such a brain for some scientists?
Who created killer weapons, human bombs and other
killer weapons
Terrorists are enjoying these weapons creating fear and
tears in people
Should the scientists go to Moon and Mars spending
Millions of rupees?
can't they do some thing to give a decent life on earth
for people to live?

Thank God
For medical scientists for producing life saving drugs and
machines
Environmental scientist who are awakening our minds to
safeguard our planet
Agricultural scientists who are developing new methods
of producing more
Nuclear scientists who wish to use nuclear power for the
benefit of people
Astrophysicists helping us to understand the solar
system

Lord, do remove selfish interests in these scientists
Educate the scientists to use science only for the welfare of
the people
Enable them not to destroy the beauty of your creation
Let the scientists join hands with you in uplifting people
Let the scientists not pollute water resources and climatic
conditions
Take charge of scientists, save your image in us and
your created universe. Amen

69. PRAYER FOR MISSIONARIES AND EVANGELISTS

God, the missionary of Missionaries
You have commissioned people to bear witness to your mission
They have committed themselves for your cause
May your love empower them to love your people
As they go through hills and valleys to meet your people
Let them be protected by your rod and your staff

Let each one of them use their tongue carefully
Let their words and deeds bring succor to the poorest of the poor
Let their attitudes be punctuated by care and compassion
Let their spirituality reflect your sacrifices for the humanity

We pray for those who are in pain and tears for proclaiming your love
Lord, transform those who are against the conversion to your path
Let those people realize their cruel sin against your people
Let no one commit any violence against any other person on any reason

We pray for the families of the missionaries and evangelists
Strengthen their devotion and dedication for your mission
Equip them with your wisdom, your care and your compassion
Let them realize that you are journeying with them always. Amen

70. PRAYER FOR CHRISTIAN INSTITUTIONS

Dear Lord Jesus Christ, who is the Lord of all institutions
We thank you for all Christian Institutions, the off-shoots of the church
Born to nurture, heal and give succor to your people
Remold bosses of the institutions to the mission framework
If they are found outside of your mission
Bring them back to be your servants to serve your people

Founders of these institutions took years of hard work to build
They conceptualized institution's work based on your teachings
Dedicated people have served these institutions for years
With lots of hope they had handed over institutions to our hands

As many institutions celebrate centuries of their existence
We bow down to you O God with gratitude to erstwhile leaders
Help us to remember the original purpose of our institutions
Make us accountable to you what ever we do in these days

Let the church and institutions work together in your fear
Let each one of them responsible for each other
Neither church nor its institutions should become boss to people
Bring them back to be servants of your people
Let your name be glorified through church and Institutions.
Amen
(This prayer is dedicated to Tercentenary Celebration of ISPCK)

71. SENSE OF GRATITUDE

(To people who played an important role in my life
formation, To institutions which shaped my life)

Bishop Henry Lazarus discovered a Pastor in me
And encouraged me to go for theological studies

Bishop Leslie Newbegin, who selected me for theological
studies
I can never forget the interview I had in his office in
Madras

Bishop L.V. Azariah taught me English grammar
I like his personality, his messages and his soft corner for
me and my family

Dr. Christopher Durai Singh's theology classes enlarged my
thinking
His theological jargon, concepts, personality made an
indelible mark on me
Dr.Russel Chandran's teachings and interpretations I
admire
I was enriched by his boldness in theological thinking
and good administration

Dietrich Bonnhoeffer's courage in protesting Hitler, inspired
me so much
His theology and his resistance movement challenged me
so many times

Hans Kung's theological interpretations have enlivened me
in theology
His interpretations are very apt and relevant to modern
times

Dr.S.J Samartha's inter-religious dialogue writings Helped me to get involved in Dialogue meetings and Inter-religious initiatives

As a student of Minjung theology under Dr. Kim Yong Bock enabled me to compare the notes with our own Dalit theology

Bishop. Ananda Rao Samuel's life style, messages, his humility made a great impression not only in my life also on my family too.

Bishop Vasantha Kumar, as a friend, mentor and Bishop gave me new life through his generous help and care

Peggy Hockings and Betty Willims of LMS in 1970s have been a great source of learning and encouragement

Institutions like Hope High School and Besant theosophical college in Madanapalle, United Theological college in Bangalore, Presbyterian Theological College and Seminary in South Korea have reformed my thinking

National Council of Churches in India, Christian conference in Asia,

World Council of Churches in Geneva have provided a forum to express and experiment my thoughts

Conferences like, World Council of Churches meet in Zimbabwe, Gospel and Culture meet of World mission in Salvador, Brazil, Common Witness programme of WCC in Bossey, Switzerland and Bangkok, Decade against Violence of WCC, and all other programmes of
National council of Churches in India have inspired And enriched me in my theological thinking.

My own pastoral ministry in Chittoor, Pakala and Chinnampall pastorates

In Vellore Diocese, KGF and Bangalore in Karnataka Central Diocese,

All saints Cathedral in Nagpur and St.John's Church in Fort, Vellore has humbled me and made it possible for me to make a greater commitment to my Lord Jesus Christ.

My ministry as radio programme producer at FEBA and my literature works with ISPCK has given me a great boost in my ministry

How can I forget my parents Yesupadam and Padmavathy
who gave their life to me and wished to see me as a Pastor
Their encouragement, prayers and sacrifices they made were foundations for my life and theological thinking and Christian values

I am grateful to my brothers and sisters and sisters-in-Law, brothers-in-law, Parents- in- Law for their co-operation and support given to me

Of course I owe so much to my wife Kasthuri for her unfathomable love, son Kiran for his great sacrifice of his kidney to me daughter Keerthi for her unreserved love and care for me innumerable friends around the world have made a great impact in my life 'to be what I am today'

What I spoke, what I did, what I sang. what I wrote what a life I lived, what travels I made, what friends I gained. What family and relatives I have, have been God's gift to me. God alone to be praised in my life.

72. MY PRAYER FOR YOU

Hallow, My dear,,
I pray for you to pray and believe in God
My God and your God are the same
My needs and your needs are almost the same
For God, you and I are the same
God will listen to your prayer as He listens to my prayer
Let us not divide the God-hood in the name of our religion
Let us pray for each other's welfare
Let us together place our situation in the loving hands of God
His answer may not be as per our will
But He will answer our prayers according to His will
May you and I enjoy life according to God's terms

Our loving and caring God,
Though we live in a confused and corrupt world
I am delighted about your presence with me and us
Deep seas, high skies, innumerable people and their cultures
Make my knees bow down in an awesome wonder and prayer
Help us to be under your reign and let your will be done
In our life, make us realize that you are with us always. Amen

73. GOD WITH US

Listening God,
In the midst of thundering noises around, can you hear me?
Seeing God,
In the midst of happening world, can you locate me?
Caring God,
In the midst of uncared tears and cries, can you not take care of me?
Weeping God,
In the midst of pain and struggles of people, can I wipe your tears?
Journeying God,
In the midst of hustle and bustle of this world, can you hold my hand?
Teaching God,
In the midst of indoctrination of faiths, can you not teach me the right?
Empowering God
In the midst of survival of the fittest, can you empower me to live?
Healing God,
In the midst of commercialization of faith, can you not reward my faith?
Beckoning God,
In the midst of demands of this world, help me listen to your call?
Just God,
In the midst of injustices haunting me, Can I experience Justice?

Comforting God,
In the midst of failures and losses, May I experience comfort in you?
Transforming God,
In the midst of the evil and corrupt world, transform me to do Good
Forgiving God,
In the midst of the sin being enjoyed, Pardon me to pardon others
Smiling God,
In the midst of all sorrows and pain, bless me with one of your smiles
Creator God,
In the midst of pollutions of all sorts, instill in me the creativity
Uniting God,
In the midst of disunity prevailing, unite all people as God's family   Amen